MW00915498

Witches Garden

To my sister Kristi, the paramedic,
thanks for checking my rough drafts
for signs of life.

Witches Garden

Written by
Laurel Lorenzini

Illustrated by
Gabriel San Martin

Copyright © 2023 Laurel Lorenzini

All rights reserved. No part of this book may be reproduced
or used in any manner without the prior written permission
of the copyright owner, except for the use of brief
quotations in a book review.

To request permissions, contact the publisher at
hello@laurellorenzini.com

Hardcover: ISBN- 978-1958817-186
Paperback: ISBN- 978-1958817-193
Ebook: ISBN- 978-1958817-209

First paperback edition: September 2023

Illustrated by: Gabriel San Martin

Contents

CHAPTER 1

Spring at Last

It was early spring, and the local witch doctor, Mags, woke up smiling. It was finally time to plant this year's garden, which was good because she was running low on medicine for the ghouls and monsters.

The sun wasn't even up yet, but Mags practically jumped out of bed, to her cat Shadow's annoyance. Over a breakfast of cutworms and oatmeal, she made a list of what she would need.

☐	Screaming strawberry plants	☐	Fiery tomatoes
☐	Blue booberry fertilizer	☐	Clam sprouts
☐	Dracula orchids	☐	Drumming asparagus
☐	Ghost plant	☐	Octopus stinkhorn
☐	Spiky cucumbers	☐	Witch Hazel

She tapped her pen against her cheek. "I should probably get extra screaming strawberries," she said to herself and underlined the first item on the list.

Mags loved planting season. The only downside was she would have to plant alone this year because her granddaughter Bo wouldn't be back for another month. Mags's heart began to race at the thought of Bo studying far away in the desert.

"Deep breath, Mags," she told herself while rubbing her rhodonite worry stone. Two months had passed, and nothing had happened to Bo. Surely she wouldn't go missing like Mags's daughter had. Only one more month to go. And springtime was finally here.

"Shadow, would you like to come with me to the nursery?" asked Mags. Shadow squinted, refusing to lift her head. "Very well, Shadow, you sleep. I'll be back soon!" Mags couldn't help but chuckle. Ever since Bo had left, Shadow's general contempt for everything and everyone had reached comical levels. Mags grabbed her broom and flew off to the local nursery.

CHAPTER 2

Crack of Dawn

"Hello Bill!" said Mags as she bustled through the door.

The vampire grinned. "Well, hello Mags. How are you this frightful night?"

"I'm well. It's good to see you. How's the family?" It had been three years since Bill had flown nearly halfway across the world to get a special plant so Mags could heal his little boy. He still had the scars from the wind burn, but Mags knew he'd do it again. Fortunately, the young vampire had been just fine after a few days of treatment.

"Good. The littlest bats are sleeping through the day now. How is Bo? Back yet?"

"Only one more month," said Mags, clapping her hands.

"You must miss her like crazy."

"I do, but she writes often, which helps a lot. And she's having a great time." Picturing her worry stone, Mags continued, "Anyways, I'm excited this winter is finally over. I could barely keep up with the demand for the Vani-flu. I need to plant more screaming strawberries this year so I can make a bigger batch."

"Ah, it's the perfect time to plant a garden. There will be a full moon at sundown."

"A most auspicious time."

"Indeed. The shop has been busy. But it's almost five a.m.: closing time. I will sleep well today I'm sure. What would you like this year? The usual?"

"Yes," she said, handing Bill her list. "Plus a few additions. Do you have any critter-catcher plants in stock? I had a hard time keeping my screaming strawberries from being eaten last year."

Bill nodded. "They are irresistible to our mammalian friends. We have some responsible critter-catchers available."

"Excellent. I will take one of those, everything on the list, and some nepeta cataria for Shadow. Also, do you have any airy-cherry-berry plants? Bo can't resist airy-cherry-berry chews."

"We do. Right over here. Look how juicy these stems are," he said, breaking off a small tip of one of the plants. "We just got them in yesterday, actually. And Shadow will love the catnip. It was grown by the mountain-cat herders." Bill whistled, and in flew Glen, his assistant. The bat Glen landed, taking the shape of a sharp-toothed human boy. Bill gave him the list and some instructions, then Glen jumped off the ground, turned back into a bat, and flew away.

Bill asked Mags, "Will you require delivery today?"

"That will not be necessary. I brought my broom-haul." Mags paid in seven wish clams, a day-sickness spell, and three protective charms. "Good dawn, Bill."

"Good dawn, Mags."

Outside, Mags expanded her broom tow and attached it to the back of her broom so Glen could pack up her purchases. A short while later, Mags was flying back home into the sunrise.

CHAPTER 3

A Witch's Garden

When Mags got home, Shadow was lying in a patch of morning sunlight. "Hi, sweet girl. Still sleeping? You missed Vampire Bill. He was working today." Shadow didn't stir. "He did have some catnip he thought you might like." Before Mags finished the sentence, Shadow was all sweetness and love, rubbing against Mags's legs. "I thought that might wake you up. Here." Mags pulled out the mountain catnip. Shadow purred gratefully.

Mags went outside, put her plants and seeds aside, and began to prepare the ground. She tilled the soil, ripping out any old roots or weeds that had already grown. She mixed lime into some topsoil. The acidity had to be just right to grow potent herbs, fruits, and vegetables.

She had already picked out a spot to work up the dirt for the extra screaming strawberries, and now she mixed the soil so it would be just perfect. Hopefully, there would be enough to make all the medicine she needed.

She worked until lunch. She was almost done, but she stopped for a needed break. It seemed she was no spring chicken anymore. *Well,* she thought, *I am one hundred and thirty-three now.* She made a sore muscle tea to drink with her centipede and pesto sandwich. Sitting under a tree, admiring her work, she drifted to sleep and dreamt of soaring through the sky in the glow of a brilliant harvest moon.

When she woke up, it was dusk. Mags popped up and quickly finished up the prep work in the garden. Then she brewed a grow spell to use that night. She showered and changed into the copper-colored robe she liked to wear when she blessed her garden.

Now she just had to wait. Breathing deeply in the night sky, she let her worries of the ghoul flu and of Bo slip away.

She accepted and released her loneliness without Bo and her longing for her daughter Miriam. She fully connected herself to nature.

When the full moon entered the sky, Mags began the grow spell. First, she said a prayer requesting the goddess above to protect her garden so she could successfully grow the things she would need to keep her community healthy. Second, she began to dance a dance of spring and life. Third, she began to plant the plants and seeds, listening to her instincts on their preference of location within the garden walls. At last, she planted the critter-catcher and cast a protection spell around her garden. She had once seen a critter-catcher capture a squirrel and fling it, terrified, over the garden wall until it landed in a dazed heap on the grass. The protection spell would keep any caught critters from harm.

With the planting done, there were only two steps left. She had to sprinkle the plants with the grow spell and do the full-moon rain dance to water the thirsty garden. Later, properly drenched from the rain, she went inside for a long peaceful sleep.

CHAPTER 4

Howling Werewolf

The next few days were busy as Mags tended the garden while keeping up with making and selling healing spells. One day, Haggle Tooth ambled toward the shop. Haggle Tooth was a very old, mostly decrepit, retired witch doctor. She stopped in the street to save a frog from a speeding bike headed its way. A witch after her own heart: Mags didn't like seeing harm come to any creatures either. Movement at her feet caught Mag's attention. The tip of a tail poked out from under the checkout counter.

A certain lizard had been living under the counter for nearly two years. It had first sneaked in to live under a shelf in the back, but when Mags had tried to introduce

herself, the lizard had screamed and pretended it was invisible. It had darted to the checkout counter, and ever since, Mags had pretended she couldn't see it. She had a great fondness for the little guy and not just because he was excellent at keeping pests away. Secretly, she thought of the lizard as Cornelius, and sometimes she "accidentally" left food and water in the shop.

The bell rang, and Haggle Tooth shuffled in, her intricate black robe, embroidered with hundreds of spiders, swished with each step.

"That's a beautiful robe, Haggle Tooth," said Mags, straightening out her own comfortable, plain purple dress.

Haggle Tooth's shoulders scrunched up. "Thanks. I'd like to purchase some wort-be-gone." Mags was momentarily confused. First off, it was one of the easiest potions to make.

Why would another witch need to buy such a thing? Secondly, Haggle Tooth had never worried about her worts before. Why start now at her age? Perhaps it was for someone else. Even more confusingly, Cornelius hissed when Haggle Tooth stepped up to the counter. It was quite unexpected. Mags had never heard Cornelius hiss before, and it broke his pretense of invisibility.

But Mags had no time to think about any of these perplexities because a howl suddenly echoed from the doorway. Clevis Clem, a werewolf, entered the shop. He was clutching his jaw and making a rumbly moaning sound. Mags had a flashback to last summer's sea witch festival when Clevis, amid a burst of laughter, had stuffed a whole bucket of chicken feet into his mouth and cracked a molar.

Apparently, the tooth was still bothering him. Clevis did not bear pain well, so Mags quickly grabbed a bottle of pale blue wort cream and handed it to Haggle Tooth. The elderly witch dropped three dried snapdragons in payment and mumbled "bye" before scooting out the door.

Mags tapped her cheek. "Am I missing something?" she asked herself. Clevis howled, distracting her. Scrambling to collect the ingredients for a mending potion, Mags never noticed the saboteur spell that crawled from

Haggle Tooth's robes across the kitchen floor. It was not until days later that Mags noticed some of her screaming strawberries were missing.

"How can this be? Critter-catcher, who got by you?" Mags asked in exasperation. The plant only shrugged its leafy stems. Mags started monitoring the garden daily. Sure enough, screaming strawberries, her most important plants, were disappearing one or two each night. The problem was, she had no clue how.

The critter-catcher was capable of answering yes and no questions via shrugs, nods, and head shakes. It assured her it had seen nothing take the strawberries, and it had been awake and on guard all night.

Mags knew it was possible for infected critter-catchers to steal the very things they should be guarding and lie about it, so she gave the critter-catcher a truth serum.

The critter-catcher was telling the truth: it had, in fact, seen nothing. She also knew a tongue-tie spell could keep someone from revealing the truth about what it had seen.

She wasn't sure such a spell would work on a critter-catcher, but she gave it a detangling remedy anyways. She learned what she already suspected. The critter-catcher was not the problem.

Rubbing her chin, Mags had one more idea. "Alright, critter-catcher, let's try an invisible print powder." She spread the powder around the garden and screaming strawberries. The powder only revealed itself after being walked on.

"Maybe this will reveal the culprit," she explained to the critter-catcher, but, unsurprisingly, it didn't respond. She tried not to feel discouraged. It felt like, they were in battle together. At least she wasn't alone—the critter-catcher was her only ally though. Mags hoped they would win. In the meantime, she had to open the shop.

The next evening, there were fewer plants but no additional footprints.

"Well, Shadow, we'll just have to watch the garden ourselves." She got a wool blanket, some pillows, and a huge thermos of Rasputin tea. They settled in for the night-long patrol at the edge of the garden and promptly fell asleep.

The next morning, Mags woke with a start. "Well, that didn't work, Shadow." Sitting up, Mags gave her back a little massage and yawned. The shop had been so busy lately, she wasn't surprised she hadn't been able to stay awake.

"After we solve this screaming strawberry mystery, we'll have to hire someone to help in the shop," Mags concluded. "We can hire an after-school helper. Maybe a young monster with multiple arms so we can get a bunch of things done at once." Shadow blinked slowly, unimpressed, but the thought made Mags smile.

CHAPTER 5

Witchlet Woes

That same sleepy morning, a young witch mom, Zee, and her two little witchlets, Sevi and Sor, entered the shop. Mags was helping two monsters in the line, so she raised her hand in greeting. Inwardly she sighed. Sevi and Sor were the two most mischievous kids in town, and she didn't want to deal with whatever disaster awaited this time.

Their mother looked harried. She was telling the witchlets, "If you behave, you can have snail-slime pops. But if you don't, I'll turn both of you into statues."

While the monsters at the front of the line debated between the spicy or sweet maggot skewers, Mags couldn't help but frown at the memory of the last time

the witchlets were in the shop. Mags had taken Zee to the back room to look at brooms, and when they'd returned, the shop had been full of young witch giggles and frolicking amphibians. Mags wasn't confident that a bribe and a threat would keep those two in line.

The girls were still looking at the pops, but the line was long. By the time it was Zee's turn, the witchlets were eyeing the shimmering insects on display behind them. Without even turning around, Zee said, "Don't even think about it."

"Hi Mags, how are you doing?"

"Good, I can't complain. How are you?"

"It's been a day, but I see that you are busy. Let me give you my order and get out of your way. I need purple stinkhorn and a vial of spiky cucumber gel."

"Alright, it'll be just a minute," said Mags. As she was collecting the stinkhorn, she heard a jar shatter, then an angrily muttered spell. By the time she turned around, the lizard who lived under the counter was running toward the spilled glowworms, tongue-out, and both witchlets were stone. One witchlet was clapping her hands with a look of glee, and the other's hand was held out to where the jar had been. Mags let out a long sigh. She got the Norwegian glowworms from a traveling troll who only came through this area in the fall, about six months from now. Mags would have to special order a delivery through Bat Express, at exorbitant costs, if she was going to replace it.

A red-faced Zee was apologizing while trying to catch the escaping worms, distracting Mags from her own anxiety. Zee was saying, "I'll pay for these of course. I'm so sorry."

Mags grabbed an empty jar. Together they caught what they could, but shimmery glow worms are surprisingly fast, and a now-glowing Cornelius had eaten most of them before running back under the counter. After they had stoppered the bottle, set the almost empty jar on the shelf, and cleaned up the glass, Zee again insisted on paying for the glow worms.

"No, no, it's alright. Really. I know witchlets can be a handful."

"Maybe I can help you in some other way?"

"Not unless you know someone who would be interested in working here part-time. It's been swamped lately. I can barely keep up."

"No, I regret I don't. If I did, I would have hired them to babysit Sevi and Sor while I got chores done today," said Zee. "When does Bo return?"

"She'll be back in a couple of weeks. But she's so busy with her studies when she's home that I really need to get some help in the shop anyways." Mags bagged up Zee's order while Zee got a thoughtful look on her face.

"I do have a cousin coming to visit. His name is Fern, and he is good with plants. Like really good. He is part plant himself. Perhaps he could help you with your garden so you have more time to prepare potions or something?"

"Really? Part plant? I do have a perplexing garden problem. My screaming strawberry plants keep disappearing, but the critter-catcher hasn't seen anything."

"That sounds right up Fern's alley. I'm sure he can give you some insight. I'll send him over in the next couple of days. He should be arriving in town tomorrow. Are you sure you won't let me pay for these worms?"

"No, no. It's alright. There are still a few left, and I think I'll just hold off ordering more until there is a call for them.

It's not a big deal. I hope you aren't too hard on the witchlets."

"No, I won't be. But they won't be getting slime-snail pops, that's for sure. Bye, Mags."

Mags watched Zee turn her girls back into flesh and blood. The looks on their faces were priceless: joy, confusion, understanding, and then shame. "Sorry Mom," they mumbled. Their mother raised an eyebrow at Mags, and the witchlets turned to her too. "Sorry Ms. Mags."

"It's Alright. Run along, girls," said Mags. Mags couldn't begrudge the witchlets when it was obvious they felt bad about what they had done and understood their actions were wrong. Before Mags had a chance to reflect on a witch being part plant (wow), another customer trooped in. Back to work.

CHAPTER 6

Plant Whisperer

A few days later, Mags was again standing before the critter-catcher. But this time she had Fern, a self-described plant whisperer, by her side.

"I didn't know it was possible to communicate with plants," Mags said.

"I have learned to tune into their acoustics," said Fern. "They are always sort of tapping away when talking. Sometimes they let out chemicals to communicate too, especially in times of danger. Of course, it helps that I am part plant. It's in my genes, so to speak. So, you are trying to find some missing fruit plants?"

"Yes, can you please ask the critter-catcher if it has seen anything out of the ordinary?"

"This will work best if you speak directly to the critter-catcher. I will interpret the answers."

Mags repeated her question to the critter-catcher and stepped back. Fern leaned closer and after a few minutes of what seemed like absolute silence, Fern turned to Mags.

"We have a problem. It seems you have offended Tom. First off, Tom says he would like to be addressed by his name, and secondly, he says you've accused him of lying twice, which he finds wounding. Tom says you might as well have cut off his branches, it hurt so much."

Taking Mags aside, Fern said, "Listen, Mags, you should know critter-catchers are proud plants. They are hard workers and will usually do their work very well but not if they are depressed. Tom will be much happier if he feels he is being treated with the utmost respect. I'd apologize if I were you. You are unlikely to get much cooperation otherwise."

"Of course! I had no idea," said Mags. Walking back to Tom, Mags said, "Tom, I am so sorry! I didn't realize you had a name. I will definitely call you Tom from now on. And I wasn't accusing you of lying. I just had to make sure you weren't infected with a lying virus or being silent from a tongue-tie spell. Clearly, I was mistaken. You are very healthy and free of any enchantments. Please accept my apology. I never meant to offend you, and I could really use your help."

With that, Fern stepped closer to Tom and cocked his head, seemingly very interested in what Tom had to say. Mags was in awe of the world just beyond general perception. A few moments later, Fern was telling Mags, "Tom accepts your apology and wants to compliment you on your balanced soil and excellent care of the garden. He respects your gardening skills. He also says that, although he has sent thirty-seven squirrels flying into the trees and scared numerous deer, birds, bunnies, and groundhogs away, only one unusual thing has been observed. The sky to the north is darker than it should be."

Mags had no idea what to do with that information, but she made sure to thank both Tom and Fern profusely. She tried to pay Fern in sunny-day spells, but he refused. "Zee would turn me to stone if I took payment. I owe her, and she said this would make us even."

"Well, if you are ever in the area again, please say hello. And if you ever need a place to work, I would be happy to employ your services. Every year this garden gets bigger, and every year I have less time to tend it."

"I'm usually not in this neck of the woods, and gardening is a little beneath my skills." Looking around, Fern added, "I'm really only here because I was asked to speak at a symposium in Bells Hop next week and Zee's is a good halfway point in my travels. But, I'll stop by on my way back home and see how you and Tom are doing."

"That would be great. I'd love to talk to you more about how you communicate with plants. And thank you again, Fern. I don't yet know what Tom's information means, but it's more than I had before. I'm sure it will be helpful." With that, Mags and Fern parted. Mags waved sadly. "Well, he'll be back," she encouraged herself. Mags went inside to ponder Tom's words over a cup of peat tea and dead-man's-finger mushroom soup.

CHAPTER 7

Creepy Crawlies

At last, Mags called her sister Florencia, a non-practicing witch doctor who spent most of her free time reading ancient spell books for fun. This is stranger than it sounds because all spellbooks are ancient by definition. What Flo read was so boring and indecipherable, most witches wouldn't even touch the books. Every few years, she would make a connection from something she'd read that would transform the witching community. She was far and away the most renowned witch doctor to make entries in Witches United Journal. Whenever Mags was out of ideas, Flo was the perfect person to call.

"Hi Flo, are you free to meet this evening?"

"Sure, I could use a break. The regular place?"

"Creepy Crawlies still makes the best moss cake."

"Alright, I'll see you in thirty minutes."

Flo was already waiting at the cafe, her commanding presence impossible to miss. Mags waved shyly, marveling at how Flo never had a hair out of place. It was hard not to feel less powerful by comparison. They embraced hello and sat down.

"I went ahead and ordered moss cakes and peat tea," said Flo.

"That's great, thanks. How have you been? I've missed you."

"I've missed you too. I've been knee-deep in ancient Egyptian doctor notes. Though the doctor in question was, in fact, a witch hired by the pharaoh himself.

The pharaoh was open-minded about witches in private but not so much in public. That's why nobody really knew who his doctor was."

"That actually sounds more interesting than your usual projects."

"Ha! I thought you might think so. It is very interesting, but it's been a strain on my eyes. I was happy to have an excuse to take a break," Flo said with a smile. "How have you been?"

"Good, the shop has been hopping."

"How is Bo?"

"She's doing great. I got a letter from her Thursday. She's invited a group of desert nomads to come visit if they are ever in the neighborhood. Where they would all stay, I don't know, but you know Bo. She doesn't worry about logistics."

"She's a bit of a wanderer herself."

"But why did she have to wander so far? What's wrong with staying in this town?"

"Not everyone is like you Mags—content in one place helping others. Traveling can be enlightening."

"You're right, of course. I learned a lot just moving out of the healing forest to this little town. I just worry about her safety."

"I know. But she isn't going to disappear like Miriam. She'll be back soon." When Mags's daughter had mysteriously disappeared, Flo was her rock. Mags couldn't even get out of bed for weeks, but Flo cared for Bo and headed a futile search.

"How's Shadow?"

"Shadow does as she pleases. She has been in a foul mood since Bo left, so there is that too."

"Yes, we all miss her." Noticing Mags's downcast face, Flo added, "At least it's springtime now. I know how you hate winter. I don't notice it as much, as my head's usually stuck in a book, but we are southern witches."

"These mountain winters chill me to the bones. I'm planning to be better prepared. I'm going to make a six-month supply of warming spells." After a bite of delicious moss cake, Mags said, "I have a problem I was hoping you could help me with."

"Sure, what is it?"

Mags explained the problem of the disappearing screaming strawberries. Once she'd finished, Flo pressed her eyes shut to think for a minute.

"Hmm, that's intriguing," said Flo, her eyes popped open. "I wonder if a Tibetan reveal spell would show what's darkening the sky."

"Tibetan reveal spell?"

"I found it last year. It's so old nobody uses it anymore and nobody accounts for protecting from it when creating a spell. Here, I'll write it down for you."

Grind fresh rhubarb with dried scorpion tail.

Flash fry it. Add lemon juice and sprinkle it around

the area in question. Then say, "Take the layers,

begin to peel, reveal, reveal, reveal, reveal."

"Thanks Flo, you never disappoint."

"Well, see if it works before thanking me. More tea?"

"Sure. Then let's take a walk on the beach, keep you out of your house and away from your books for a few extra minutes." Anticipating Flo would say she was too busy, Mags added, "You don't want to turn into dad, getting vampire-pale because you only go out when forced to."

"Okay, okay. I will agree to this, but only because it's the best time of day for a sea monster sighting. I heard there is one in the bay, and I'm determined to figure out what animal it is."

CHAPTER 8

Green Mist Bay

When Mags got home, she immediately tried the reveal spell.

Her mouth dropped open as a huge spider popped into view on the garden wall. It had been invisible because it was under a saboteur spell.

"Of course! Saboteur spells can take many shapes. That's why they are so hard to recognize. It's brilliant really."

"But I can't believe this. Can you, Tom? Shadow? Who would put such a spell on me?" Mags's joy at finally having the mystery solved was overshadowed by a sense of betrayal. Someone was intentionally doing this to her. She had moved to Green Mist Bay for a fresh start when Bo was just a toddler. Mags had done nothing

to hurt anyone. An ache sprang up in her chest, and she slumped against the garden wall trying to make sense of it. Rubbing her worry stone she murmured, "All I do is try to help this community. I don't understand."

But then Shadow curled up on her feet and Tom patted her shoulder, comforting her.

"Thanks guys." It reminded her of all the loved ones in her life. She took a deep breath and sat up straighter. "I'll just have to do what I can now and get to what I don't know later. For now, I will make a de-saboteur potion and clean this spell up."

That night, while brewing cedar bark stew, Mags saw a small black spider walk across the mantel. It reminded her of Haggle Tooth's black robes. Suddenly, Haggle Tooth's strange purchase made sense.

"Haggle Tooth!" she shouted in triumph earning a startled glare from Shadow. "It's Haggle Tooth's saboteur spell! And I bet she put a spell on Clevis to create a distraction too! I have the how and the who but not the why." She tapped her cheek. "Why did she do it? Tomorrow I will be paying dear Haggle Tooth a visit!" Shadow stood, arched, and turned her back on Mags as a final objection to the outburst. Mags hugged Shadow, despite Shadow's annoyance. As soon as Mags let go, Shadow settled back down in a huff.

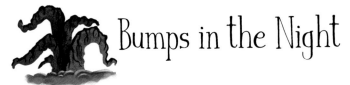 Bumps in the Night

Early the next morning, Mags heard noises coming from the shop below her apartment. Shadow was as alert and alarmed as Mags felt.

"Let's go investigate," Mags whispered.

Shadow lowered her head and feigned sleep.

"You know I know you are awake."

Shadow did not stir.

"Fine, I'll go myself." Mags's heart was pounding as she grabbed her worry stone and began sneaking downstairs to the kitchen. But before she made it two steps, Bo rounded the kitchen corner onto the stairs.

"Grammy! Sorry! I tried to be quiet, but I dropped a bag." Shadow darted out of Mags's room, ran down the stairs, and immediately started purring and rubbing against Bo. All smiles, Bo crouched to snuggle the cat. "Hi, Shadow. I missed you too."

"Bo! I'm so happy to see you. Is your semester abroad finally over?"

Laughing, Bo said, "Yes Grammy. I just got off the train. I missed you."

With a big embrace, Mags said, "I missed you too. And I love your hair!"

"Thank you. It's a rainbow— get it? Since my name is Bo?"

"Very clever. It suits you. Are you hungry?"

"Starving."

"You go unpack. I'll make us some breakfast."

"Grammy, I need to tell you something. I kind of adopted a pet. Or he adopted me." Mags raised her eyebrows in surprise.

Bo sang out, "Blaze, come here." A small, mottled dragon flew to Bo's shoulder. Shadow hissed and jumped to the top of the stairs.

Bo explained, "Blaze is a desert dragon. I met him shortly after some humans captured his mother. I saw the whole thing but couldn't save her. I was barely in time to stop them from taking Blaze too. Anyways, we've been inseparable since. I hope you don't mind. He is mostly fire trained."

Mags couldn't help but smile. "Why not? It's a house of misfits, what's one more? That's sad about his mom though." Normally such a story would depress Mags but not today.

Today she had Bo back. All she wanted was for Bo to live in a warm, loving environment where she was safe. Although she had to admit, a fire-breathing dragon in a flammable house didn't sound particularly safe.

"Are you sure you aren't mad?"

"Goodness, you still look young when you want something. Are you really seventeen now?" Mags tapped her chin thoughtfully. "Bo, when I lost your mom, I learned something. If I can't embrace the unpredictable events life offers, I might as well be fertilizer. And really, who could have predicted you bringing a dragon back from your semester in the desert?"

Turning to Blaze, Mags said, "Welcome to your new home, Blaze." Blaze gave Mags a toothy grin. From the top of the stairs, Shadow hissed and walked away with her tail in the air.

"It might take a while for Blaze to win over Shadow, though."

Mags put on some music and made a feast: ant frittata, algae pancakes with passionfruit jam, fresh gooseberry juice, and eighty-six-grain bread. Everything seemed better when Bo was around.

"Grammy, why are you listening to sea shanties? I thought you didn't like the local music?"

"You're right, but I guess it is growing on me. Or I'm just really happy. Let's eat."

Over breakfast, Bo described the cave paintings, sand magic, energized salts, and so on that she'd discovered, as well as the new friends she'd made during her semester abroad. Blaze happily circled the kitchen, only once setting fire to the curtain above the sink. Shadow stayed under Mags's chair, as far from Blaze as she could be while still in the same room.

Appraising her granddaughter, Mags realized something. "You seem really happy, Bo."

"I am." She smiled back. "The experience was good for me. I feel surer of myself, if that makes sense."

"That's great to hear. I suppose you going away was worth it after all."

"We should visit the desert together sometime."

"Oh. I think I'm better off here. Think of me as your home base, a place you can rest between adventures."

"You're a healing station to more than just me. Anything interesting happen while I was gone?"

Mags told Bo about everything that had transpired. Bo was especially interested in Fern because she had met a shaman who spoke highly of the desert plant people. She was excited to write to the shaman about Fern. When Mags told Bo she was planning to confront Haggle Tooth, Bo wanted to go with her. Mags agreed gratefully.

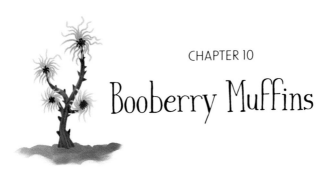

CHAPTER 10

Booberry Muffins

After breakfast, the four of them flew down the long dirt road to Haggle Tooth's cottage. Now that Bo was back, even Shadow tagged along, though she kept one eye on Blaze at all times.

Bo asked, "Isn't it weird there are no warning alarms to announce our arrival at Haggle Tooth's?"

"Very. Only the weakest of witches or the poorest wouldn't have a basic protective alarm in place. And clearly, Haggle Tooth has not lost her powers." Mags frowned, then took a deep breath. She still had to confront the elderly witch. She rubbed her worry stone. Bo smiled encouragingly, and Mags felt her courage return.

Mags marched right to the crooked door of a dilapidated cottage. Bo stayed back, giving them space to talk. Shadow sniffed around the overgrown bushes at the side of the house, and Blaze curled in a ball in the sun to sleep. Mags knocked.

When Haggle Tooth saw who was at the door, her eyes grew wide. Before the other witch could say anything, Mags accused, "You put a saboteur spell on me!" Feeling she had been too harsh she lowered her hand and quietly asked, "Why?"

Haggle Tooth visibly deflated, sighed, and explained, "You've taken all my business."

"I thought you retired years ago," replied Mags.

"I work part-time," she said. "Or at least I did until you ran me out of business." Haggle Tooth sat down in a rickety old chair on the veranda. She motioned to the empty seat, and Mags sat.

"Oh, Bo, come sit. You might as well hear this too," sighed Haggle Tooth.

Bo sat as Shadow disappeared around the side of the house.

"I'm sorry. I should have tried talking to you, Mags. I thought if you didn't have enough screaming strawberries, customers would be forced to come to me for help. I don't have enough money for food or maintenance of my cottage."

"I didn't know," stated Mags. Haggle Tooth looked very tired, as tired as Mags had been feeling lately. "If I had known, I would have shared the customers with you."

Then Bo chimed in, "Why don't you guys work together? You keep saying you've been so swamped, Grammy."

Both Mags and Haggle Tooth stared at her, mouths open, but then Mags thought about it. "That's actually a brilliant idea." Turning to Haggle Tooth she said, "Come work with me! I really am swamped, and I've seen firsthand your skill at spellcasting. You clearly know your stuff."

Haggle Tooth gulped. "I tried to sabotage you! And I'm old."

"I know, but I need help, and you need work," Mags said eagerly. She was already imagining what fun it would be to have company and how nice it would be to take breaks. "Your age doesn't matter. Maybe you could work behind the counter or make spells in the kitchen. We will figure it out. I just need you to promise to use your words to work out any problems you have with me. No more secret spells. What do you think?"

"Of course. I would love that. But now I feel worse than ever. You should be reporting me for violating the B.R.E.W. (Basic Rules of Ethics in Witchery), not offering me a job.

I truly am sorry, Mags. I didn't know what to do." Gesturing, Haggle Tooth confided, "Even my poor cat Eclipse has been suffering. He is always forced to find his own food. I get some angry looks from him on those rainy, cold winter days."

Chuckling, Mags replied, "Attitude is something I am very familiar with when it comes to cats."

"Let me show you something." Haggle-Tooth stood and ambled around the side of the house. Eclipse opened one eye to watch them. When Mags and Bo turned the corner, they saw a beautifully maintained garden. It looked out of place with the rest of the house and yard. The garden was divided into two, and there were two signs. One said, "Screaming Strawberries," and the other said, "Mags's Screaming Strawberries."

"I kept all your strawberry plants separate. I had hoped to return yours to you someday. You can have them all back, of course, and you can use mine too.

I also noticed there are quite a few spells you don't sell. I could make them for your shop."

"That would be great, Haggle-Tooth."

Blaze flew over the garden.

"Oh, that's a beautiful desert dragon," Haggle Tooth marveled. "Where did he come from?"

"He's new to our family. Kind of like you," said Mags.

Haggle Tooth grinned crookedly. "I don't have a new friends spell on hand, but I do have peat tea and booberry muffins inside."

"I believe that works just as well," said Mags, smiling.

"Sounds good to me," said Bo. "I love booberry muffins!"

"Please, come in," Haggle Tooth said, one crooked tooth peeking out of her smile. "And thank you both."

Coming Soon:

Witches Garden Chaos